Where IS Happy?

This book belongs to:

• •

Text by Louise Shanagher
Design and illustration by Rose Finerty

Where Is Happy?

THE LILLIPUT PRESS
62–63 Sitric Road, Arbour Hill
Dublin 7, Ireland
www.lilliputpress.ie

ISBN 978 1 84351 729 0

10 9 8 7 6 5 4 3 2 1

This is the second book in the Mindfully Me series.

Printed in Spain by Castuera

A Note for Parents and Teachers

This book encourages children to practise finding peace and happiness within themselves. It also prompts children to question whether external things such as toys and sweets really bring lasting happiness. The story promotes self-compassion, self-confidence and self-esteem by encouraging children to love and accept themselves just as they are, to think positively about themselves and to be a good friend to themselves.

How to use this book

You can use the text and pictures of this book with children to initiate conversations about what makes them feel happy. You can ask the children questions such as 'Do you think it is important to have lots of toys?' or 'What do you think about being cool?' This can help you gain a deeper insight into the children's inner worlds, their opinions, thoughts and feelings.

When you have finished reading the story, you can ask the children to put their hands on their heart and to say to themselves 'I am perfect just as I am.' You can show them the pictures on the last page of the story and ask them to give themselves a big hug, then spread their arms and legs out wide to 'shine like a star'. It works well to do these actions along with the children. You can tell them that they can practise this sequence any time they like.

This book introduces four simple and effective tools which promote children's positive mental health.

Positive affirmations

Articulating positive affirmations is an effective method of encouraging positive self-talk and self-esteem. The story encourages children to practise affirmations such as 'I love to be me.' You can create affirmations to suit children's specific needs.

Self-compassion

The story encourages children to have an accepting and compassionate attitude towards themselves. The action of putting your hand on your heart and giving yourself a hug has been proven to reduce stress and promote self-compassion. You can encourage children to practise these actions.

Mirror work

This book introduces mirror work to children, which is a wonderful tool that promotes a positive self-image. Children can practise this using any mirror at home. As children look in the mirror, they can say 'I'm perfect just as I am.'

Power posing

On the last page of the story, the children stand in a star pose. This is called a 'power pose' and has been proven to increase confidence and reduce stress if it is held for two minutes or longer. You can encourage children to hold the pose by doing it along with them and holding it while listening to their favourite song.

How to use the workbook pages

You can use the workbook pages to reinforce the message of the story and to help initiate conversations about thoughts, feelings and experiences with the children. Try to create an accepting and non-judgmental atmosphere as you help the children with the workbook pages. Reassure the children that there are no right or wrong answers: all our thoughts and feelings are OK. By talking about them, we can get to know ourselves better. Children can write or draw their answers into a 'mindfulness diary' that can be used every day as a way for children to express their feelings.

Younger children may be more comfortable talking through their responses rather than writing or drawing them. The Mindfully Me series is aimed at children aged four and up, and additional ideas for activities for different age groups up to eight years old can be found at **www.loulourose.net**.

Tips for teachers

This book is aligned with the Irish primary schools' SPHE curriculum and the Aistear framework. The book links particularly well with the strand 'Myself' and the strand units 'Self Identity' and 'Growing and Changing'. For tips on how to use this book in the classroom, lesson plans and other resources please visit **www.loulourose.net**.

would you like to join us on our quest to find
Happy?

where do you think we
might find it?

will we have to
look far?

you might be in for
a surprise ...

where does Happy come from?
Does it come from diamond rings?
Does it come from looking gorgeous
or having lots of shiny things?

Where can I find Happy?
Can I buy it in a shop?
Does it come from being clever,
or by eating sweets non-stop?

Where does Happy come from?
Does it come from a new bike?
Does it come from being popular
or eating all the cake you like?

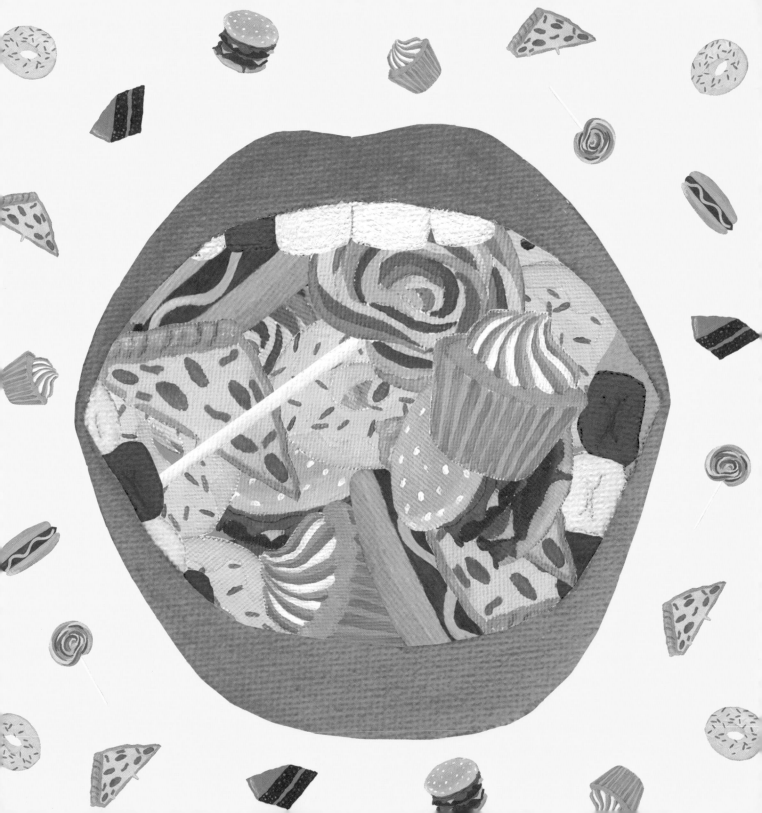

No, all these things are nice to have but only last so long.

Happy is a place inside, to know this makes you strong.

yes, Happy comes from inside,
comes from deep inside your heart,
comes from knowing that you're special,
loving each and every part.

yes, Happy comes from inside,
you don't have to look far.
From believing that
you're brilliant
to accepting all you are.

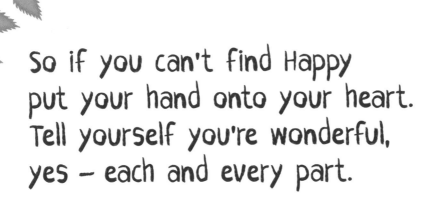

So if you can't find Happy
put your hand onto your heart.
Tell yourself you're wonderful,
yes — each and every part.

Remember that you're perfect,
just the way you are.
Give yourself a great big hug
and shine just like a star.

Shine just like a star!

All About Me

It is very important to be a good friend to yourself.
Colour in the picture and give yourself a big hug.

Thinking Good Thoughts

Thinking good thoughts about ourselves help us feel happy inside. Finish these sentences and talk about them with a friend or an adult.

I was really kind when _____

_____

_____

One of the best things about being me is _____

_____

_____

Something I'm proud of is _____

_____

_____

I love myself because _____

_____

Things I Like About Me

write about, draw or stick in a picture of something
that makes you happy to be you.